Read all the titles in this series

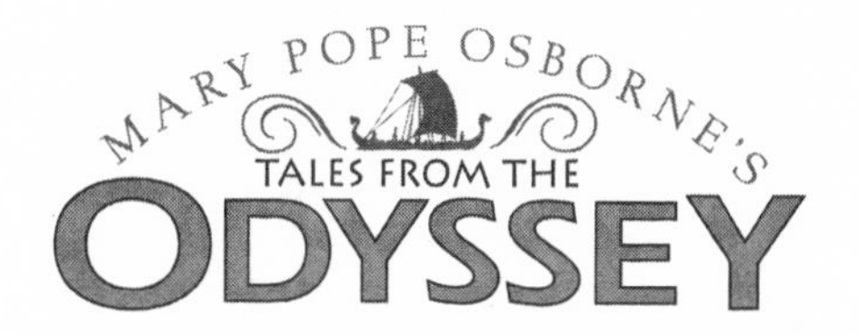

BOOK ONE
THE ONE-EYED GIANT

BOOK TWO
THE LAND OF THE DEAD

BOOK THREE
SIRENS AND SEA MONSTERS

BOOK FOUR
THE GRAY-EYED GODDESS

coming soon:
BOOK FIVE
RETURN TO ITHACA

BOOK SIX
THE FINAL BATTLE

Circe's Island
The Sirens
Island of Aeolus
Scylla
Cyclops' Cave
Island of the Sun God
Charybdis
Land of the Dead
Calypso's Island
Land of the Lotus Eaters
Oceanus

Map of Odysseus' Journey

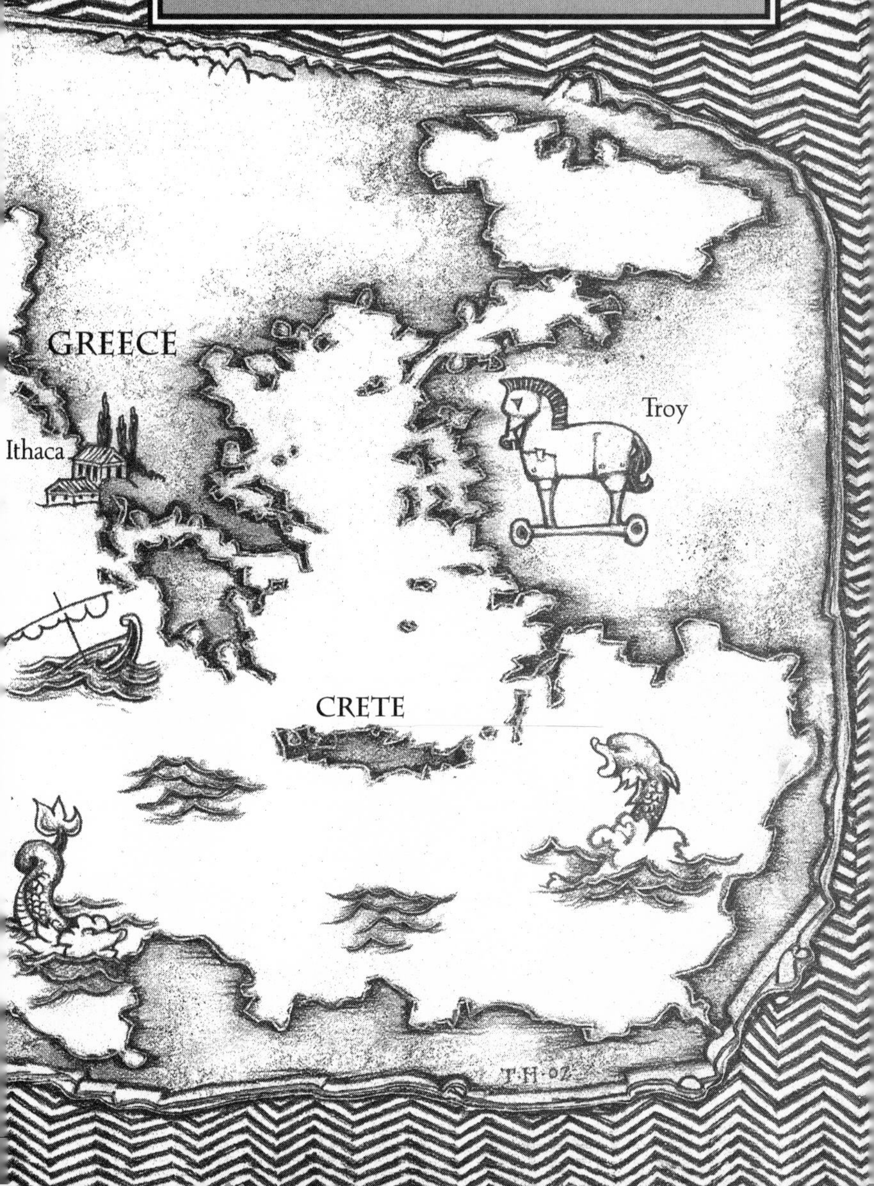

MARY POPE OSBORNE'S TALES FROM THE ODYSSEY

T·H·02

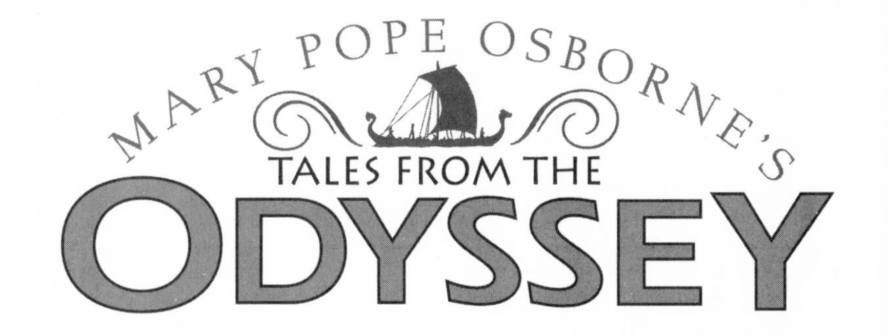

Book Two

THE LAND OF THE DEAD

By MARY POPE OSBORNE
With artwork by TROY HOWELL

Hyperion Paperbacks for Children • New York

Special thanks to Frederick J. Booth, Ph.D.,
Professor of Classical Studies, Seton Hall University,
for his expert advice

First Hyperion Paperback edition, 2003
1 3 5 7 9 10 8 6 4 2
Printed in the United States of America
Library of Congress Cataloging-in-Publication Data on file.
ISBN 0-7868-0929-9 (pbk.)
Visit www.hyperionchildrensbooks.com

For Eric Booth and Le Clanche du Rand

CONTENTS

PROLOGUE

In the early morning of time, there existed a mysterious world called Mount Olympus. Hidden behind a veil of clouds, this world was never swept by winds, nor washed by rains. Those who lived on Mount Olympus never grew old; they never died. They were not humans. They were the mighty gods and goddesses of ancient Greece.

The Olympian gods and goddesses had great power over the lives of the humans who lived on earth below. Their anger once caused a man named Odysseus to wander the seas for many long years, trying to find his way home.

Almost three thousand years ago, a Greek poet named Homer first told the story of Odysseus' journey. Since that time, storytellers have told the strange and wondrous tale again and again. We call that story the Odyssey.

ONE

ISLAND OF THE CANNIBAL GIANTS

For days, Odysseus, king of the Greek island of Ithaca, rowed with his warriors over the calm sea. As he rowed, Odysseus felt great pity for his men. He knew they

through a narrow passage. They tied their ships together near the shore. Though the waters were calm and peaceful, Odysseus felt a strange foreboding. He ordered the crew of his own ship not to moor their vessel with the others, but to anchor it near the mouth of the cove.

When the Greeks had gone ashore, Odysseus climbed a rock to look out over the strange land. He saw the smoke of a fire rising in the distance. *Who lives here?* he wondered.

He quickly returned to his men and

ordered three of them to climb over the cliffs and explore the land.

"Find out who lives here," he said. "Tell them we wish them no harm."

The three scouts set out at once. Odysseus and the others waited on the rocky shore for their return.

The men had not been gone long when horrible screams filled the air. Two of the scouts charged down the side of the mountain. Shrieking and waving their arms, they appeared to have gone mad.

"What has happened?" Odysseus shouted.

In trembling voices, the men told their terrible tale.

"We met a girl at a spring—she invited us to go with her," one said. "When we entered her house, her mother appeared—a hideous giantess—"

"Tall as a mountain!" cried the other. "She sent for her husband—another giant—a cannibal!"

The men broke down, sobbing. They told how the cannibal giant had snatched up their friend and eaten him before their very eyes.

A roar then shook the harbor like thunder.

Odysseus looked up and saw a legion of giants standing at the top of the cliffs.

The bloodthirsty cannibals began picking up huge rocks. They hurled them down the mountainside.

"Board the ships!" Odysseus called to his men. "Set sail at once!"

As the other Greeks scrambled onto their ships, Odysseus and his crew ran toward the mouth of the cove where Odysseus' black ship was moored.

The rest of the fleet was doomed. The giants hurled their rocks down upon the ships docked in the harbor. The rocks smashed the vessels to splinters and crushed many of the sailors to death.

As the Greeks screamed in agony, the cannibals raced down to the shore and speared men as if they were catching fish for supper.

Watching with rage and horror, Odysseus knew he could save only the men aboard his own ship. He drew his sword and slashed the anchor rope.

"Row! Row with all your might!" he shouted to his men. "Row for your lives!"

As the screams and cries of their comrades filled the air, Odysseus and his crew frantically rowed away from the cove of the cannibal giants.

giants spearing the helpless wounded.

Finally, the black ship came upon an island covered with thickets and dense woods. The Greeks climbed ashore and collapsed on the rocky beach.

For two days and two nights, Odysseus and his men lay on the hard ground, mourning their lost comrades.

On the third day, when rosy dawn crept over the island, Odysseus gathered his strength and stood up. He did not wake his crew, for he knew they had lost all heart.

They are too stricken with grief to hunt for

food, he thought. *Soon they will be too weak to sail, and they will die on this island.*

Desperate to save his men, Odysseus picked up his sword and spear. Then he set out in search of game.

Odysseus climbed a craggy hill and looked about for signs of life. In the distance, he saw smoke rising from the green forest. It curled above the trees and drifted into the sky. *Did more giants and monsters live on this shore?* Odysseus wondered anxiously. *Or might the inhabitants be welcoming and kind?*

Before Odysseus could answer these

questions, he knew he must find food for his men.

The gods seemed to hear Odysseus' thoughts—for just then, from out of the trees walked a giant stag with towering antlers.

Odysseus hurled his spear, killing the stag at once. He then fashioned a rope from willow twigs and tied the legs of the stag together. He hoisted the stag onto his shoulders and carried it back to the Greek camp.

Odysseus found his men huddled in a circle, their cloaks wrapped around their heads. Still deep in mourning, they wept bitter tears for their fallen shipmates. They trembled for their own fate as well.

"Listen, my friends," said Odysseus. "You and I shall not go down to the Land of the Dead this morning. It is not our day to die. Until that day comes, we must take care of ourselves. Rise. Be well. Let us feast on this gift from the gods."

The men uncovered their heads. They admired the mighty stag Odysseus had slain for them, and slowly they began preparing for their feast.

They washed their hands and faces in the sea. After many days of grief and suffering, their hearts began to mend.

THREE

THE WITCH'S SPELL

All afternoon, Odysseus and his crew feasted on deer meat and wine. When the sun set and darkness covered the island, they lay down on the shore and slept peacefully.

At dawn, Odysseus roused his men.

"Friends, I do not know where we are," he said. "I know only that we are on an island. Yesterday morning, when I went hunting, I climbed a hill and saw the sea all around us. I know that others live here, for I saw smoke rising from the heart of the forest—"

Before Odysseus could go on, his men cried out. They feared that more horrors like the Cyclops and the cannibal giants might await them on this strange shore.

"Harness your fears!" Odysseus commanded. "We have no choice but to explore this island. We know not where we are or how to find our way home. We must seek help from strangers."

Odysseus' men paid no heed to his words. They only grew more anxious. Before they surrendered completely to their terror, Odysseus came up with a plan.

"Listen to me," he said. "We will form two groups. I will be captain of one, and brave Eurylochus will be captain of the other."

Odysseus quickly divided his men. Twenty-two Greeks were placed under his own command, and twenty-two under that of his trusted warrior, Eurylochus.

"Now Eurylochus and I will cast lots to see which of us will explore the island," said Odysseus.

Odysseus and Eurylochus cast lots in a helmet. The lot fell upon Eurylochus. He had no choice but to lead his men into the heart of the green forest.

With great dismay, twenty-two Greeks lined up behind Eurylochus. Some wept as they marched away through the shadowy trees, fearing their impending death.

The Greeks who stayed behind wept as well. So many of their friends had already been slain that they readily imagined they might soon lose more.

Hour after hour, Odysseus waited for the return of Eurylochus and his band of men. He watched the shadows of the forest and listened for their voices. He feared he might have made a great mistake by forcing them to set out on their quest. But he dared not share his fears with the men who had remained behind.

As the sun was setting over the island, Odysseus finally heard the tramping of feet. Eurylochus burst from the trees. He was alone. His eyes were wide with terror.

Odysseus and the others rushed forward to hear his story. But Eurylochus collapsed on the ground, shaking and moaning, unable to speak.

Odysseus grabbed him by the shoulders and pulled him to his feet. "Where are the others?" he cried. "Why did you leave them?"

Eurylochus could not answer.

Odysseus shook him again. "Tell us!" he demanded. "Are they dead?"

"No—not dead," said Eurylochus. "Worse! Worse than dead—" He broke down, weeping.

"Tell us what happened!" Odysseus demanded again.

In a shaky voice, Eurylochus told his tale: "We traveled through the forest until we came to a valley. We saw a gleaming stone wall. We stepped through a gate into a clearing, and soon came face-to-face with huge wolves and mountain lions with long, sharp claws!"

"You were attacked by these wild creatures?" Odysseus asked.

Eurylochus shook his head. "They did not attack us," he said. "The wolves licked us and whined like pet dogs. The lions gently pawed us and mewed like house cats. It was strange and unnatural. We should have turned back—"

Eurylochus trembled and covered his face. But Odysseus shook him again. "Go on with your tale," he ordered. "Tell us what happened next."

Eurylochus continued. "We were frightened to be greeted so strangely by these creatures," he said. "We moved quickly past them to the inner courtyard of a palace. A voice rang out from a window—a woman singing. She had the most beautiful voice I have ever heard."

"Who was she?" asked Odysseus.

"I do not know," said Eurylochus. "When we peered through the window, we saw a radiant being weaving at a loom. She looked like a goddess. She had long braids that shone in the sunlight. Her gown was made of jewels that seemed to change colors as she sang. She wove a cloth made from the most delicate silken thread.

"I wanted to lead us away at once, for I thought of all the terrible dangers we had faced on our journey. But I alone seemed worried. The others called out to her, and she came to her door and invited them in. I held back, hiding, while they rushed forward to enter her home. I could not stop them—they followed her into her house, and she closed the door behind them.

"Peering secretly through a window, I saw her offer them food and wine. Then she turned her back on them, and she mixed a potion of pale honey and wine. As she poured this into their food, I called out to warn them. I feared she was trying to drug them. But the men seemed not to hear—they swallowed her potion willingly.

"In an instant, they were transformed. They knew not where they were or how they'd gotten there. They could not remember one another's names—or even their own. While they were in this state, the woman tapped each of them with a wand. And suddenly, they—"

Eurylochus trembled at the memory.

He hid his face, and a chill went through Odysseus. What horrible thing had the witch done to his men?

Eurylochus looked up at Odysseus. He caught his breath, then finished his dreadful tale.

"Bristles sprang out all over each man's body," he said. "They began to snort and grunt like pigs. Their heads turned into pigs' heads."

The Greeks cried out and drew back in horror.

"The enchantress then herded the pigmen into a pigsty," Eurylochus said. "She threw acorns and butternuts to the ground, and they greedily gobbled them up like . . . like swine in a farmyard!"

For a long moment, Odysseus stared at Eurylochus in silence. Finally, he spoke calmly and decisively. "Take me there," he said. "Show me the way."

Eurylochus cried out in anguish. He threw himself at Odysseus' feet and begged for his life.

"No, no! Never again!" he cried. "Let us escape this cursed island now—before the she-monster bewitches us all!"

Odysseus saw that he could not calm

Eurylochus' fears. But neither could he abandon his comrades trapped in the pigsty of the beautiful witch.

"Very well, stay here and rest with the others," he said. "In truth, I am the leader of all the Greeks on this island. I must save my men. I will find the way alone."

FOUR

THE MESSENGER GOD

Odysseus slung his bronze sword over his shoulder. His men watched with great distress as he left their camp and headed off into the woods.

Odysseus walked through the quiet

green forest, through shadow and light, past gnarled trees and dense brush, until finally he came to the valley. In the distance rose the gleaming stone walls of the witch's palace.

Odysseus halted. For a moment, he thought of turning back. But he quickly gathered his strength and moved boldly toward the gate.

Suddenly a young man stepped into his path.

Odysseus started to reach for his sword. But in an instant, he realized this was no ordinary human. The man was radiant. He shone with a light so bright that Odysseus was forced to looked away.

"Your courage is admirable, Odysseus," said the stranger. "But do you know who your enemy is? Have you never heard of Circe the enchantress, daughter of the sun and the sea?"

Odysseus sighed with despair. He had indeed heard of Circe the enchantress. He knew that as a mortal, he had no power to escape her charms. Once he entered her palace, he would certainly be put under a spell like the rest.

"Do not despair, Odysseus," said the

stranger. "I have come to help you conquer Circe and free your men. Will you not trust Hermes?"

Odysseus looked up. Could this truly be Hermes, the messenger god of Mount Olympus, son of Zeus, and protector of heroes and travelers?

"I bring a charm to protect you from the witch's spell," said Hermes.

"What is it?" breathed Odysseus.

"A special herb, impossible for humans to unearth," said Hermes. "Only the gods can take it from the ground."

The god reached into a bag and pulled

out a black-rooted herb with a flower as white as milk.

"The gods call the flower *moly*," he said. "Eat the moly, and it will protect you from anything that Circe gives you to eat or drink. When she taps you with her wand, draw your sword and make her swear an oath not to harm you."

Hermes handed the black-rooted herb to Odysseus. Then, without a word, the shining god turned and disappeared back into the green forest.

Odysseus stared after Hermes in wonder. Until now on his journey,

Odysseus had only angered the gods—the warrior goddess, Athena; the sea god, Poseidon; and the wind god, Aeolus. Were the gods looking upon him with favor again?

Odysseus looked down at the magic moly in his hands. He raised the flower to his lips and ate it. Then, with new strength and courage, he walked toward the gleaming walls of the witch's palace.

FIVE

THE WITCH'S PALACE

Odysseus opened the gate that led to Circe's palace. Huge wolves and lions prowled the courtyard. The animals approached him eagerly, sniffing the air and making soft, friendly sounds.

Odysseus stared at them with horror and pity. He knew that they were men trapped in the bodies of wild creatures.

Odysseus moved swiftly through the courtyard. At the door of the palace, he called out for Circe.

Soon the enchantress appeared. Her long braids gleamed like gold. Her jeweled gown shimmered and sparkled.

She spoke in a soft, warm voice. "Enter, please," she said to Odysseus, and she held open the door.

Without a word, Odysseus stepped

into the sunlit palace. Circe invited him to sit down and rest.

"Let me make a drink to refresh you after your long travels," she said.

She left the room for a moment. Then she came back with a cup, and she handed it to Odysseus.

"Here," she said. "Drink this."

Odysseus put the cup to his lips. As he sipped the brew, Circe tapped him with her wand.

"Foolish man!" she said. "Off to the pigsty with the rest of them!"

Hermes' magic herb protected Odysseus

from Circe's evil spell. He did not turn into a pig as the witch had expected. Instead, he pulled out his bronze sword and held it to her throat.

Circe shrieked in alarm. "Why does my magic have no effect on you?" she cried. "Who are you? What is your name?"

"My name is Odysseus," he told her.

"Odysseus!" she said. "Hermes once told me that a great warrior named Odysseus would someday visit my palace. If you are indeed this man, put away your sword! We must trust one another and become friends."

Odysseus glared at her. "How can you speak of trust when your evil magic has transformed my men into beasts? You must swear an oath that you will do nothing to harm me."

Circe bowed her head. In a whisper she swore not to harm Odysseus. When Odysseus put his sword away, she called for her handmaidens.

Lovely nymphs of the woods and rivers slipped out from the shadows of the palace. They made a great fire under a huge cauldron of water.

Odysseus bathed in the soft, healing

waters. Then he dressed in a flowing cloak. The nymphs led him to the great hall of the palace where a feast had been prepared for him.

Circe invited Odysseus to sit at her table. She filled their golden cups with wine.

But Odysseus would not eat or drink. He sat in silence, staring at Circe.

"Odysseus, why will you not eat my bread or drink my wine?" she asked. "You must not fear me now, for I have given my solemn oath that I will never harm you."

Odysseus fixed his eyes upon her.

"What sort of captain could enjoy meat or wine when his men are not free?" he asked. "If you want me to be happy at your table, you must undo the spell you have cast over my men."

Circe held his gaze for a long moment. Then she took a deep breath and rose from the table. With her wand in her hand, she stepped out of the palace into the courtyard.

Odysseus followed her and watched her open the gate to the pigsty. Twenty-two fat pink hogs barreled forward, snorting and grunting.

The enchantress rubbed a potion on the head of each animal, then touched them all with her wand. All at once their bristles fell off, and the pigs miraculously turned back into men. The men were younger, taller, and more handsome than ever before. They embraced Odysseus and wept with joy. They asked about their comrades.

Even Circe was moved by the tears of her captives. "Odysseus, go back to the rest of your crew. Bring them to my palace," she said. "I swear that I will treat them well, too."

Odysseus left the palace. He hurried through the green forest until he came to the men waiting for him on the shore. When they saw their leader alive, they shouted with great relief and threw their arms around him.

"With the help of Hermes, the spell of Circe, the enchantress, has been broken," said Odysseus. "Your comrades have all been turned back into men. Come with me now to the palace and you shall be united with them."

Some of the Greeks drew back in fear.

"I assure you," Odysseus told them

gently, "Circe has sworn to welcome you into her palace."

All the men finally agreed to go with Odysseus. They pulled their ship onto the shore and hid all their belongings in a cave. Then they followed Odysseus back through the shadowy green forest until they came to Circe's glimmering palace.

Circe welcomed the Greeks into her palace. She bid her handmaidens to draw baths for the men and anoint them with olive oil. The nymphs gave the tired Greeks woolen cloaks and tunics, then led them to a feast in the great hall.

At the feast, Circe urged Odysseus to remain with her in her palace. "You are not the same man you were when you left Ithaca long ago," she said. "Your battles and sorrows have left you weak and weary. Your own family will not know you."

Odysseus did indeed feel a great weariness as he thought of the war with Troy and his nightmarish voyage toward home—the monsters and giants, the cruel deaths of his men.

"Stay with me until you have forgotten all your grief and sad memories," said

Circe. "When you are strong in mind and body, I will help you find your way home."

Feeling the burden of his losses, Odysseus surrendered to the wishes of the lovely witch. He promised Circe he would stay with her until he and his men were strong again.

SIX

ANOTHER JOURNEY

In the days that followed, Odysseus and his men enjoyed the warmth and luxury of Circe's palace. They rested and ate good meat and drank sweet wine.

As they refreshed themselves on the

enchanted island, time passed swiftly. The days turned into weeks, and the weeks into months. After a full year, Odysseus' men came to him.

"Should we not leave this palace soon?" one asked.

"Have you forgotten Ithaca?" said another. "Shall we never see our homeland again?"

Odysseus' heart was stirred by the words of his men. He thought of home—of Penelope and Telemachus, and of his mother and father. A great yearning to see them rose up in him.

He hurried to Circe's chambers.

"My men and I are strong again thanks to your kindness," he said. "But remember the promise you made me? You said you would help us return safely to Ithaca, once we had rested and regained our strength."

"And I shall," said Circe. "But you must take another journey first. You must seek counsel from Tiresias, the blind prophet of Thebes. Tiresias sees the future. Only he can tell you how to get home."

"But Tiresias of Thebes is dead," said Odysseus, puzzled.

"Yes, Tiresias is dead," said Circe, "but he still has all the wisdom he had on earth."

"I do not understand," said Odysseus. "How can one who lives in the Land of the Dead give counsel to a living man?"

"You must travel to the Land of the Dead," said Circe. "There you will speak to the ghost of Tiresias."

Odysseus could not speak. It seemed an unbearable terror for a living man to visit the dark world ruled by the god Hades, and his queen, Persephone.

"No man has ever found the Land of the Dead," he said in a hushed voice.

"Only the spirits know how to travel there. What ship will take me? What wind will blow?"

"You cannot travel all the way there in your ship," said Circe. "The North Wind will take you to the edge of the sea, to Oceanus, the river that circles the world. Once you have sailed across Oceanus, you may enter the Land of the Dead."

"What must I do then?" Odysseus asked.

"You must disembark from your ship and travel on foot through a grove of willows and poplars," said Circe. "When you come to the place where two rivers meet—the River of Groans and the River of Flame—dig a trench. Pour honey, milk, wine, and white barley meal into it, as gifts to the spirits of the dead. Then sacrifice two sheep and pour their blood into the trench. After you have done this, stand guard until the ghost of Tiresias appears. Allow him to drink from the trench, and he will tell you how to find your way home to Ithaca."

Odysseus bowed his head. He knew he could not avoid this dreadful journey if he wanted to see his home and family again.

He tried to gather his courage, as he so often ordered his men to do. He looked up at Circe and nodded.

Then, without another word, Odysseus pulled on a fine cloak and strode through the palace, waking each of his men.

"Rise now," Odysseus said. "We must leave this place today."

The men were relieved, for they imagined they were about to set sail for home. But when the Greeks had gathered outside the palace, Odysseus revealed their true destination.

"Soon we will set sail for Ithaca," he

said. "But first we must go on another journey. We must travel to the Land of the Dead. There I will speak with the ghost of the wise prophet Tiresias."

The men cried out in protest. But Odysseus told them he had no choice.

"Only Tiresias can tell me how to find the way home," he said. "Please, come with me. Give me company on my journey to the Land of the Dead."

Their heads bowed in anguish, the men followed their leader down to their ship. They climbed aboard. They hoisted their sails and pushed out to sea.

As the black ship sailed over the waves, Odysseus felt a gust of warm gentle wind. He sensed that Circe was close by.

The enchantress sent fresh breezes all day. She filled the sails of the black ship and sent it flying over the waves.

SEVEN

THE LAND OF THE DEAD

When the sun had gone down and darkness had fallen, Odysseus and his men arrived at the edge of the sea. They sailed through a gray mist into the deep waters of Oceanus, the river that flows around the world. Then they sailed across Oceanus and finally came to the Land of the Dead.

The Greeks moored their vessel on a dark riverbank shrouded in fog. As they stared into the mist, the men shook with terror, afraid to venture into the haunted realm. Odysseus himself trembled at the thought of what lay ahead. But with firm resolve, he stepped ashore and ordered his men to follow him with two sheep from Circe's island.

Odysseus and his men traveled on foot through a grove of poplars and willows. They stopped when they came to the place where two rivers met, the River of Flame and the River of Groans.

There, in a place never touched by the rays of the sun, Odysseus dug a deep trench. He poured in the mixture of honey, milk, wine, and white barley meal. He offered prayers for the spirits of the dead. Then he ordered his men to slay the two sheep as a sacrifice to the gods.

As soon as Odysseus poured the blood of the sacrificed animals into the trench, ghostly beings appeared out of the mist—the spirits of old men and women, the spirits of warriors still wearing their armor, the spirits of young women who had mourned for their lost men and died of broken hearts.

Thousands of ghosts began moving slowly toward the Greeks. Drawn to the scent of the blood, they made strange wailing noises.

Odysseus' men shook and trembled. Odysseus himself turned pale with fear. But he drew his sword to keep the spirits away until the ghost of Tiresias, the blind prophet, appeared.

While Odysseus fiercely guarded the trench, his gaze came to rest on one of the spirits floating through the mist. With shock and horror, he recognized someone he loved very dearly.

Moving toward him was the ghost of his own mother.

EIGHT

LIKE A SHADOW OR A DREAM

Odysseus wept. He had not seen his mother for more than ten years, not since he had left Ithaca. He knew now that one of his worst fears had been realized—while he had been away, his beloved mother had died.

He called her name. But the spirit of his mother did not speak to him—she did not seem even to recognize him. She seemed only to yearn for a taste of the sheep's blood in the trench.

In spite of his great sorrow, Odysseus held up his sword and would not let his mother's ghost come closer. He kept guarding the trench, waiting for the spirit of Tiresias to appear.

At last a frail figure drifted out of the mist. Carrying a golden scepter in his hand, the ghost of an old man moved through the swirling gray air toward the animal blood. Odysseus lowered his sword and allowed the spirit of Tiresias to drink from the trench.

Once the ghost had had his fill of the sheep's blood, he rose and turned to Odysseus. In a clear, cold voice, he said:

"Odysseus, you have come to ask me about your journey home. The gods are making your voyage very difficult. They will not allow you to escape the anger of Poseidon for blinding his son, the Cyclops."

Odysseus felt a wave of despair. The

curse of the Cyclops seemed too terrible for him to endure.

"Do not lose hope," the ghost said. "You may still return to Ithaca. But you must heed my warning. On your way home, you will pass the island of the sun god. On this island there are many beautiful sheep and cattle. Do not let your men touch even one of these creatures. They are much adored by the sun. Any man who tries to slay them will meet his doom."

Odysseus nodded.

"Tell your men to leave these herds

untouched and think only of returning home," the ghost said. "If they do not obey this command, they will die, and your ship will be destroyed. You alone might escape. But if you do, you will be a broken man. And you will find great trouble in your house."

Odysseus was grateful for the wise man's warnings. He resolved to keep his men from touching the cattle and sheep of the sun god.

"Many years from now, death shall come to you from the sea," the ghost of the soothsayer said finally. "Your life shall leave you when you are old and have found peace of mind."

Odysseus nodded. "If this is the will of the gods, so be it," he said. As Tiresias started to move away, Odysseus called after him. "Wait, please, before you leave—"

The ghost turned back.

"Can you tell me why my mother's spirit does not speak to me when I call her name?" Odysseus asked.

"Your mother's ghost can speak only if you allow her to taste the blood in the trench," answered the ghost of Tiresias.

"Until then, she has not life enough to speak."

The spirit of the wise prophet turned away and Odysseus watched him fade back into the mist.

Odysseus then bid his mother's ghost to come forward and taste the blood from the trench.

Once she had tasted the sheep's blood, the spirit of Odysseus' mother seemed to gain strength. When she looked again at her son, she cried out in surprise.

"My beloved!" she said. "You are not a spirit! Why are you here?"

Odysseus gently explained to his mother the reason for his journey to the Land of the Dead. Then he asked her many questions: "How are Penelope and Telemachus? Did Penelope bury my memory and marry another? How is my father? Is he still alive?"

The ghost looked at her son sadly.

"Your family has been broken by sorrow," she said. "Your wife still waits for you. But she spends her days and nights weeping. Your son is strong and brave. Though he is young, he guards your home, your fields, and your livestock. He also mourns your absence, as does your father. Your father lives in the country and never goes near town. In winter, he wears only rags and sleeps on the floor. In summer, he sleeps in the vineyard. He weeps for you all the time."

Odysseus was grieved to hear this news of his family. "And you, Mother?" he asked. "What sad fate has befallen you?"

"Your absence weighed too greatly on my heart," she said. "As I grew more and more certain you would never return home, I became too sad to live."

Odysseus reached out to embrace his mother's ghost. Three times he tried. But each time, she slipped away from him as if she were made of air.

"Mother!" he cried. "Why are you not there when I try to embrace you?"

"My son, I am only a spirit," she said gently. "Leave the Land of the Dead, now. Find the light of day while you still live."

To Odysseus' great sadness, the spirit of his mother then faded from his sight, like a shadow or a dream.

NINE

THE WARRIOR GHOSTS

When the ghost of Odysseus' mother had gone, more spirits came forward to drink from the trench.

Odysseus drew his sword and ordered them to approach one at a time.

First came the spirits of the wives and the mothers of slain Greek heroes. Then came the ghosts of the great kings and warriors themselves. Among them was the ghost of Agamemnon, High King of the Greek forces during the Trojan war.

"My lord, king of us all!" Odysseus cried. "You are here!"

As soon as he had tasted the sheep's blood, Agamemnon recognized Odysseus. He tried to lift his arms to embrace him, but there was little strength or power left in his ghostly being.

Odysseus wept tears of pity. Until now he had not known that Agamemnon had died. Now they sat and talked with one another—the living man on one side of the trench, and the ghost of the mighty king on the other.

"What fate brought you here?" asked Odysseus. "Did you drown in a terrible storm at sea? Did an enemy strike you down in some great fight?"

Agamemnon told Odysseus that he had been slain by his own queen.

"But you will not meet the same end, Odysseus," the ghost of Agamemnon assured him. "Your wife, Penelope, is loyal to you. She is a most admirable woman. When you left her, she was little more than a girl. When you return, she and your son will be waiting to embrace you and work with you on your farm."

As Odysseus and the spirit of Agamemnon sat weeping and talking, the ghosts of warriors came and sat with them, warriors who had fought valiantly in the Trojan war. Among them was great Achilles, the bravest of all the Greeks.

"Odysseus, what a daring thing you do now," said Achilles. "Why have you traveled here to be with the ghosts of the dead?"

Odysseus told Achilles and the others about his journey and how he had come to meet with the ghost of Tiresias. He praised Achilles, calling him a prince among the dead.

"Ah, perhaps," said Achilles, "but I would rather be a poor man's servant in the world of the living than a king of kings in the Land of the Dead."

The ghosts of other dead warriors each

told Odysseus their sad tales. And to each ghost, Odysseus gave news about the living.

Then Odysseus saw Tantalus, a king whose great pride had angered the gods. Their punishment for him was eternal hunger and thirst. Tantalus was forced to stand in water up to his chin, with fruit trees drooping overhead, their branches laden with pears, apples, and figs.

Whenever Tantalus lowered his head to drink the water, the water dried up. When he reached up to clutch the fruit, the wind blew the branches into the air.

Next Odysseus saw Sisyphus, a cruel king whom the gods had condemned to forever roll a huge rock uphill. Every time Sisyphus reached the top of the hill, the rock rolled back down the slope, and Sisyphus had to start all over again.

Odysseus then saw the mighty Heracles. The great warrior stared into the distance, holding his bow in his hands, his arrow on the string. For all time he would stand poised to take aim.

As Odysseus looked through the mist for the spirits of more heroes, he saw that thousands of ghosts were moving slowly toward him. Their voices were soft at first. Then they grew louder and louder. The spirits were crowding close around Odysseus, crying out for his help.

Odysseus felt a wave of panic. In terror, he turned and fled from the spirits of the dead. His men followed him back through Persephone's grove until they came to their ship.

Odysseus led the way on board and ordered the Greeks to set sail at once.

The men rowed swiftly across the river of Oceanus. They kept rowing until they felt a breeze and opened their sails.

As dawn's rosy light glittered on the wine-dark sea, Odysseus finally caught his breath. His mind roamed over the past year—the nightmare of the cannibal giants, the long stay in Circe's palace, and his visit to the haunted realm of Hades and Persephone.

Odysseus grieved for his dead mother and felt more anxious than ever to see his father before the old man also died. More than anything, he longed to be reunited with his loving wife and son before harm came to them.

Odysseus' heart ached almost more

than he could bear. Still, he rejoiced that he was in the world of the living and not trapped forever in the dark Land of the Dead.

ABOUT HOMER AND THE *ODYSSEY*

Long ago, the ancient Greeks believed that the world was ruled by a number of powerful gods and goddesses. Stories about the gods and goddesses are called the Greek myths. The myths were probably first told as a way to explain things in nature—such as weather, volcanoes, and constellations. They were also recited as entertainment.

The first written record of the Greek myths comes from a blind poet named Homer. Homer lived almost three thousand years ago. Many believe that Homer was the author of the world's two most famous epic poems: the *Iliad* and the *Odyssey*. The *Iliad* is the story of the Trojan War. The *Odyssey* tells about the long journey of Odysseus, king of an island called Ithaca. The tale concerns Odysseus' adventures on his way home from the Trojan War.

To tell his tales, Homer seems to have drawn upon a combination of his own imagination and Greek myths that had been passed down by word of mouth. A bit of actual history may have also gone into Homer's stories; there is archaeological evidence to suggest that the story of the Trojan War was based on a war fought about five hundred years before Homer's time.

Over the centuries, Homer's *Odyssey* has greatly influenced the literature of the Western world.

GODS AND GODDESSES OF ANCIENT GREECE

The most powerful of all the Greek gods and goddesses was Zeus, the thunder god. Zeus ruled the heavens and the mortal world from a misty mountaintop known as Mount Olympus. The main Greek gods and goddesses were all relatives of Zeus. His brother Poseidon was ruler of the seas, and his brother Hades was ruler of the underworld. Among his many children were the gods Apollo, Mars, and Hermes, and the goddesses Aphrodite, Athena, and Artemis.

The gods and goddesses of Mount Olympus not only inhabited their mountaintop but also visited the earth, involving themselves in the daily activities of mortals such as Odysseus.

THE MAIN GODS AND GODDESSES AND PRONUNCIATION OF THEIR NAMES

Zeus (zyoos), king of the gods, god of thunder

Poseidon (poh-SY-don), brother of Zeus, god of seas and rivers

Hades (HAY-deez), brother of Zeus, king of the Land of the Dead

Hera (HEE-rah), wife of Zeus, queen of the gods and goddesses

Hestia (HES-tee-ah), sister of Zeus, goddess of the hearth

Athena (ah-THEE-nah), daughter of Zeus, goddess of wisdom and war, arts and crafts

Demeter (dee-MEE-tur), goddess of crops and the harvest, mother of Persephone

Aphrodite (ah-froh-DY-tee), daughter of Zeus, goddess of love and beauty

Artemis (AR-tem-is), daughter of Zeus, goddess of the hunt

Ares (AIR-eez), son of Zeus, god of war

Apollo (ah-POL-oh), god of the sun, music, and poetry

Hermes (HUR-meez), son of Zeus, messenger god, a trickster

Hephaestus (heh-FEES-tus), son of Hera, god of the forge

Persephone (pur-SEF-oh-nee), daughter of Zeus, wife of Hades and queen of the Land of the Dead

Dionysus (dy-oh-NY-sus), god of wine and madness

PRONUNCIATION GUIDE TO OTHER PROPER NAMES

Achilles (ah-KIL-eez)

Aeolus (EE-oh-lus)

Agamemnon (ag-ah-MEM-non)

Circe (SIR-see)

Eurylochus (yoo-RIH-loh-kus)

Heracles (HER-ah-kleez)

Ithaca (ITH-ah-kah)

Odysseus (oh-DIS-yoos)

Penelope (pen-EL-oh-pee)

Polyphemus (pah-lih-FEE-mus)

Sisyphus (SIS-ih-fus)

Tantalus (TAN-tah-lus)

Telemachus (tel-EM-ah-kus)

Tiresias (ty-REE-sih-us)

Trojans (TROH-junz)

A NOTE ON THE SOURCES

The story of the *Odyssey* was originally written down in the ancient Greek language. Since that time there have been countless translations of Homer's story into other languages. I consulted a number of English translations, including those written by Alexander Pope, Samuel Butler, Andrew Lang, W.H.D. Rouse,

Edith Hamilton, Robert Fitzgerald, Allen Mandelbaum, and Robert Fagles.

Homer's *Odyssey* is divided into twenty-four books. The second volume of *Tales from the Odyssey* was derived from books ten and eleven of Homer's *Odyssey.*

ABOUT THE AUTHOR

MARY POPE OSBORNE is the author of the best-selling Magic Tree House series. She has also written many acclaimed historical novels and retellings of myths and folk-tales, including *Kate and the Beanstalk* and *New York's Bravest.* She lives with her husband in New York City and Connecticut.

Zeus
Hera
Artemis
Hephaestus
Apollo
Athena
Ares

GODS and GODDESSES of ANCIENT GREECE
Hermes
Dionysus
Aphrodite
Hestia
Demeter
Persephone
Poseidon
Hades